How to get rid of unwanted house guests

A CHRISTMAS CHILLER
SHORT STORY BY A.J. KIRBY

This is a White House Press Publication

Cover image: 'Christmas Carolers' by Darren Hester and reproduced under Creative Commons License.

ISBN: 1519646992

ISBN-13: 978-1519646996

ALSO BY THIS AUTHOR

Novels

Small Man Syndrome (Forthcoming)
The Lost Boys of Prometheus City (Forthcoming)
The Sleep of Reason Produces Monsters
A Man Could Lose Himself
Things Won't Fix
When Elephants walk through the Gorbals
Paint this Town Red
Bully
Perfect World
Sharkways.

Novellas

The Gavel
Nu-Gen
Hangingstone
Blink
Teeth
Ace Cameron and the Red Peril
Shouting into an Empty Cave
Bed Peace
The Haunting of Annie Nicol
The Black Book.

Short Fiction Collections

Trickier & Treatier
Mix Tape.

HOW TO GET RID OF UNWANTED HOUSE GUESTS

HOW TO GET RID OF UNWANTED
HOUSE GUESTS

Crooked between the sink and the breakfast bar with a tall stool digging into her back, Lynn leans closer to the window. Raises a trembling hand and slowly v's her fingers between two of the horizontal blinds. Gasps when she sees *them*, still rampantly *here* on the lawn. One of them shouts something – has he seen her? - and her heart yoyos. She almost falls over the stool in her haste to shut the blinds.

Once again she fumbles to take the kitchen phone from its cradle on the wall. Jerkily lifts it to her ear and receives the jarring monotone of the dead-line signal as a reward. This time she doesn't bother returning the phone handset to its cradle. Her hope thermometer is running absolute zero now – she won't be rescued, *they* will obdurately remain - and something like meek submission begins to ice her veins.

She's not slept in two nights and the world has sagged at the edges, like an undercooked Christmas cake pulled out the tin too early. The monotony of fear has made her, and her senses, invertebrate. And yet she knows, solidly, *they* are here. She knows for a fact now that *they* are not spectres at the feast. *They* are here, and they are expectant. And *they* will not carry on this siege indefinitely. She can hear the growling of very real stomachs, the visceral mutterings of impatience, from here. The unwanted guests won't be pacified much longer and she must give in to their will.

She wipes her hands on her apron, as though attempting to wipe away consequence, and gets back to work. The breakfast bar is covered with mountains of flour, molehills of currants. The bag of sugar slouches against the scales, crying grains. Two wooden spoons are crossed like a stake ready to be plunged into some unsuspecting heart should *they* enter here too soon. Used baking trays from her previous aborted efforts fill the sink so fully, so hugely, that it looks like some kind of canal boat disaster between two locks.

She is trying desperately to figure out how to make figgy pudding. Delia won't tell her. Nor will Nigella. And the internet's down so Jamie and Gordon are, for once, silent as well. Still, she melts a knob of butter in a blackened pan. It fizzes delicately and it seems a remarkable contrast to the feral sounds from outside. From outside, she can hear coarse talk and bawdy laughter. She can't hear the exact words – doesn't want to – but she knows from the tone that *they* are discussing things she wouldn't have discussed in her house. She can hear the clink of bottles and of glasses. Earlier there was a chorus of *Ein Prosit*, the German Octoberfest song. They are like Vikings returned from their raping and pillaging and they have made her garden their mead hall. There is a fire, over by the garden waste bin. Lynn fears that the reason it may be blazing so fiercely might have something to do with the summer house, which, last time she dared check, was looking decidedly lop-sided. They've erected trestle tables onto which they are banging knives and forks in a very insistent manner. Further away, a topiary of tents rustle by the hedgerow which separates her garden from one of the most exclusive golf courses in the north west.

Mike would have kittens. If the members of the golf club saw tents and figured he'd gone west and had suddenly allowed his garden to become a nesting place for travellers, he'd be black-balled quicker than you can say *pigs in blanket*. But Mike is not here. Mike's company Lexus is parked at the end of the driveway, on the wrong side of the siege. When he came home, late, that first night and they were here, he tried to march on up the crunchy gravel driveway, bristling with self-righteous fury. But *they* beat him back with crackerjoke pitchforks and *their* own list of demands. Mike is now probably safely ensconced on *his* stool at the bar of the Red Lion, waiting it out. Mike is the type of person won't negotiate with terrorists or kidnappers.

Lynn is just about to crack an egg into the pan when she hears the first gruff bars of the singing. It is the same song as it has always been. She's heard it something like a million times now and each time, the voices have grown more and more hoarse. But she knows they won't lose their voices. That would be too much like luck, like wishful thinking. Her hand closes around the smoothness of the egg and it feels as though she has the world in her fingers and she could crush it. Each verse-chorus-refrain driving her deeper into the snowdrift of madness.

If only she'd never answered the door in the first place.

The Saturday before Christmas was always her favourite day of the year. It was the day to decorate the tree which Mike would lug home like some jobbing lumberjack, like he'd just made man in the woods for a morning like he wasn't a security salesman at all. When the children were still here they'd help her. Then it was draping tinsel off each and every surface, even in the front room which was mostly reserved for best. Hanging a wreath on the front door. Dangling a ticker-tape string of dainty little lights around the windows and wrapping it around the banister on the stairs. This year, she'd made like she had every other year since the children had left, and had pretended there was nothing missing. A couple of eggnogs early doors had done something to fill up that gaping hole in her, but it was only when she'd heard the carollers approaching the front door, commencing with a loud rendition of *We wish you a Merry Christmas,* that she thought she might really be able to get into that all important Christmas spirit, just as she had in all those Christmases she used to know.

She'd dropped what she was doing – tucking a decorative holly leaf into the corner of the framed sampler which read 'A home without a cat is just a house' and deciding that yes, they could very well replace Mister Tomkins, it *wasn't* cruel to take on a cat which might, just might, outlive them – and scurried through into the hallway. Thinking, *I hope Mike's left some spare change in the key bowl on the cabinet because these carollers won't be doing it out of the simple goodness of their hearts.* Also thinking how good these carollers were. How professional. Not like the scraps of boys who came round in their twos and threes in their hoodies and their trainers and mumbled something by Cliff and then held their hands out for their due. No, *these* carollers were singing in the deep bass tones which, for her, were inextricably linked with Wales, with singing miners and fishermen and the like. These were tones which insinuated their way into her lower stomach, where the butterflies had long lain dormant. Tom Jones used to get her in exactly the same place. When she heard Tom sing *The Green, Green Grass of Home* it was as though that whole butterfly aviary inside her took flight all at once. Same here.

She listened a moment, just enjoying it for what it was, a moment, her forehead pressed against the lukewarm wood of the front door. Picking out the detail in the song now. For instance, when the carollers sung *wish*, *they* sung that particular word with extra gusto, a second-helping of vehemence, and it was as though *they* truly believed in wishes. As though *they* believed wishes were more than simply unspoken desires whispered in the darkness, fragile as snow. It was as though, for *them*, wishes were demands. And part of Lynn liked that.

Holding her breath in anticipation, Lynn unbolted the two deadlocks on the door. With an eye to decency, she kept the door on the chain, edging it open in instalments, just in case.

The singing promptly stopped.

Lynn wanted to urge them to continue, but her seldom heard encouraging words soon stopped in her throat like an unchewed mince pie once she saw the sheer weight of numbers out there. A herd of Fair Isle sweaters crowded the steps to the front door. *They* were knitted so close together that Lynn couldn't see the joins, so that *they* might have been sections of the same elaborate pattern. Because of this, she couldn't be sure exactly how many of *them* there were. She *thought* there were fourteen, fifteen. But that may have been a conservative estimate. This rugby scrum might have contained the trainers and the management staff too.

And *they* were like a rugby team. For a start, all of *them* were men, and all of *them* were large. *They* were broad-shouldered and bowling-ball headed and *they* were all jowly and red-faced. But on closer view, *they* were a more mature crowd than she'd first imagined. She took in wisps of grey in beards and receding hairlines. The evidence of rotundity in *their* bellies. Indeed, the more Lynn regarded *them*, the more she was convinced *they* looked like Santa on a down-day, when he'd done away with his workaday red scrubs and was perhaps gearing up for a couple of scoops down at the golf club's nineteenth hole. Some of *them* were carrying lanterns on poles, others clutched candles out before them like *they* were offerings at some Yuletide altar. One of *them* chugged a collection tub in a scarily bellicose fashion.

For an achingly long moment, this was the only sound. The carollers stared at her expectantly. She stared back at *them*, worriedly.

And then the chugger launched back into the song, and soon all of these men joined in, each now taking a new part, adding their own timbre to the overall black forest of the piece. Soon *they* were belting out the words. 'Now! Bring us some figgy pudding,' *they* chanted. As though it was an order or a Jedi mind-trick. As though if *they* repeated it enough, she would obey *them*.

And that was when she first began to feel afraid. When she looked at *their* faces. Took in how *they* sung with smiles, somehow, though the smiles never reached *their* eyes. How really, the song was a threat. This was soon to

become unalterably clear to her as the next verse began, and *they* began to bellow their warning into her face:
'We won't go until we've got some.'

And almost as soon as Lynn had it set in her head that these men were not here for good or to pecker her spirits up, as soon as she'd allowed herself to tread on the thin ice of uncertainty and that ice cracked and she'd plunged into immediate and heart-stabbing icy terror, *they* proved her right. The carollers began to edge their way up the six low stairs towards her like a pack of well-fed zombies, and suddenly Lynn's nerves were up and at 'em and before she could remind herself that really she was meek and mild, she'd slammed the door right in their faces and was punching home locks and kicking the draft-snake into place and cursing the fact Mike was bloody late once a-bloody-gain. For good measure, and because fear and loathing had spiced her blood to such an extent she *had to do something,* she'd also jammed the hallway chair under the door handle.

And then she'd stood there panting, thinking, while the singing outside got louder and louder. So loud that the echoes of it seemed to thrum up through her feet and into her desperate hands and twitchy fingers. So that it seemed the sounds were reverberating up to her from the very bowels of the earth.

She'd kicked off her house shoes. For some reason she didn't want *them* to hear her as she slipped into the front room. *Them* knowing where she was, what she was doing just about scared the baubles out of her.

She needed a drink.

At the drinks cabinet, she fumbled Mike's key into the lock after six, seven aborted attempts. Bit her lip. Then pulled out the whisky decanter and Mike's preferred crystal tumbler. The one with the CCTV camera engraved in the glass. He won it at the big security conference a few years back. Best salesman. With fingers a-tremor, she pulled the stopper out of the whisky, and at that precise second, the singing stopped. It was as though god had jammed his fat thumb down on the pause button of his celestial remote. It was also as though the pack outside had scented the whisky from afar. As though *they* were sharks and *they*'d smelled her miles-away terror-curdled blood. And Lynn almost let the decanter slide out of her hands.

'Oh God,' she whispered to herself, to god, to Santa, and it sounded too loud in the sterile atmosphere of the front room. And then, as the hairs on the back of her neck rose like strands of tinsel in reaction to heat, she felt something, her sixth sense perhaps, alerting her to something else which was out of kilter.

Her eyes were slowly, inexorably drawn to the bay window. She thought she might have seen the suggestion of movement out of the corner of her eye. And as she turned to face the horror full-on, a round face announced itself, squashing large red features against the glass, leaving snail-trails of snot or condensation against Pinnacle double-glazing.

Summoning the last reserves of her strength, she bolted to the window and drew the curtains. Then made similar sketches at the blinds and curtains of every window, or other, miscellaneous orifice of the house. Before slinking back down to the front room and fixing a double measure of Mike's whisky and curling on the sofa in a foetal, cat-like comma.

She'd remained like that for the whole of the first night and had only been drawn out of it by the new sounds from outside. She'd edged open the curtains and been greeted with the sight of the initial morning glory erections of what was to become their military-style camp. And *they* sung while *they* worked, so that her brain felt like the new-laid turf in the garden with a tent pole hammered into it.

And whenever she'd thought she might finally be able to give in to the weariness which swept over her like gravy, and which rusted her joints as though it was stuffing, *they'd* begun to sing again. Lynn didn't think it was possible to hate a Christmas song as much as she did, even if you worked in a high street store and they played *Now Christmas* from September. At least there was a bit of variety in *Now Christmas*. A bit of Wizzard to set off the Slade, a twist of Chris De Burgh as an antedote to Maria Carey.

Lynn feels something gloopy running through her fingers and belatedly looks down to see she has crushed the egg in her palm. Sections of shell have cracked off and plunged into the well melted butter and now appear to be in the process of being welded to the bottom of the pan. Quickly she turns off the heat and wipes her hands down on her apron.

Outside, *they* pipe up with another verse-chorus-refrain of *We wish you a Merry Christmas,* and Lynn desperately tries to recall her history. How long is it that sieges last? How do they usually end? Has she the time or patience, or, damn it, the bravery, to starve the unwanted guests out of her garden? Will she allow the garden to be sacked, and after it, the house? These men, these carolers, will eat her out of house and home. She recalls her personal history too: is this the worst Christmas ever?

And then she thinks *no more Mrs. Nice Guy*. The time for deliberation has passed. She begins to cook again and this time she uses a new recipe. She calls this one *How to get rid of Unwanted Guests*. You take one measure of bleach whisked up liberally with egg. You take flour, and sugar, and you cut it up with rat poison. You take mouldy teabags and bacteria-laced, unknowable foodstuffs from the food waste bin and their brown limpness can be said to resemble figs. You mix the ingredients well and whack in the oven at a temperature which matches the burning fires in hell.

And then, when your 'figgy pudding' is ready, you carry it to the front door and you call, in your chirpiest voice, *grub's up,* and you watch those men, those expectant men, gobble it down. And then you fix yourself another measure of Mike's whisky and settle down to watch a good filum on telly. After Boxing Day, you might give the Cat's Protection a call. But for now, just enjoy the silence.

Who says Christmas is a time for all the family? All that noise, all that mayhem they bring with them, don't you just feel that huge weight off your shoulders *when they finally get gone, taking all their crap with them? When they finally depart, but only after they've drunk all your booze and snaffled down all your food...* Well why not hurry the whole damned thing along a little?

Your home is your castle, and it won't do for it to be under siege. It's not selfish to desire a little peace and quiet. It's not somehow *anti* the Christmas spirit. It's just human nature.

THE END

SNEAK PREVIEW OF THE OPENING STANZA OF A.J. KIRBY'S FORTHCOMING NEW NOVEL 'THE LOST BOYS OF PROMETHEUS CITY'

Looking back, the bubble burst the night Carl got the bouncers to beat seven shades of shit out of those two lads, Neanderthals really, outside The Townhouse. But actually, it might have been earlier. Still, that was the night I realised there was no turning back for us and that everything had changed. It wasn't fun any more.

Before that night, it was the best of times.

This was us: every night like we were on camera; every night like we were stars of our own show and fat millions were tuning in to watch us. Everything we did was deliberate, and if it wasn't we made it look that way.

Cabs would drop us off at the bottom of Call Lane. We didn't have to take cabs; we were only coming down from City Square. But it was all about our image. How we'd *de-cab*. Everyone watching us. Business-cazj Carl in his pink contrast-collar shirt; dollar-sign cuff-links; watch as large as a sun-dial. Aviators. Adam, who despite the Leodian cold would have changed into a tight white tee which showed off his biceps and his tan. Me, in whatever clothes Ace had had in their window display that week. (Tonight, a nice new tan coat; black jeans; some clunky shoes which looked half Desert-Boot and which I now wasn't entirely sure about, though in the shop mirrors, they'd looked all kinds of boss.)

Call Lane. Rampant with skinny jeans and complicated hairstyles. Constellations of neon shining out from the bars and vomit running down the gutters. Bouncers, calling one-in, one-out, and Johnny Yellow, as much a Leeds institution as the football team, walking up and down the queues, strumming his guitar and singing nonsense lyrics, entertaining those unlucky enough to have to wait. Not us, of course. We knew people. Had bouncers calling us over, trying to get us in Norman or Oporto or Jake's. They were all like: 'evening, Carlo' and 'hey, Adamski!' and 'yo, Neal!'

The bouncers who let on to us were, without

exception, wearing black bomber jackets which, had you got the balls to spin them about a one-eighty, you'd see were all branded with the legend SAS. They weren't Special Air Service, of course. They worked for a kind of bouncer's co-operative which was named Safe and Secure. (And if you *had* spun them around, they'd have knocked you into the next millennium.)

We were friendly enough with them. Maybe went over to this one or that one to share a word (acting like we were superstars on a meet-and-greet with our adoring public; actually I suppose we treated them like *roadies*) but we ignored their invitations and eventually walked on, past the Corn Exchange, round the corner, and onto Assembly Street and our place: The Townhouse.

Cordons would be opened and we'd step inside like invited vampires. Catcalls and complaints from the queue outside would follow us over the threshold and up three flights of stairs. But by the time we reached the top, the air was more refined. Warmer too. Generally, we lived life closer to the sun than most. Sometimes we got blinded by it. We lived the high-life. By day, we worked on the top floor of One City Square; by night, the top floors of clubs. Then back to bed at our penthouses.

We were forever looking down on everyone else.

We knew it, too, deep down.

Still, despite the above-it-all atmosphere, it was always busy at the top of the stairs; girls who'd spent a week getting ready trying to talk their way inside the VIP section. Fellas pretending they knew a man who knew a man and couldn't they come in? Look, they had money, if that was what it took? Pointing at VIPs, riddling the bouncers this: *what's he got that I haven't?* And everyone who was anyone knew the answer.

Sometimes Adam or Carl – and sometimes me, who am I trying to kid? - would throw a bone *(fnar!)* to one of the girls. Link her arm and guide her past the Safe and Secure bouncer – this one was even wearing an SAS armband of the type a captain might wear in football - and into the promised land. And of course, she'd be all kinds of grateful and of course, if she stayed the course, she'd make it up to us back at one of our penthouses.

That night, the night Carl got the bouncers to beat seven shades of shit out of those two lads outside, we took one each. They seemed to come as a threesome so what the hell? They were hanging, kind of on the outskirts of the general melee, pretending to be more interested in something on one of their phones (a crappy brick-like thing none of us would have been seen dead with). Something about them screamed trouble, but they were the types Carl always went for. They looked plenty old enough, at least (some of the others in here were all kinds of underage). So what was it about them immediately made me think *steer clear?*

I think it was the air of bald desperation which clung to them. They were so hungry for something better that they didn't even recognise the sleaze pouring off Carl like cigar smoke. He went over and asked one of them for a light and she pulled out a cheapo lighter she must have bought from one of those ten-for-a-quid stalls on the market. Give the girl ten years and she'd probably be working one of those stalls.

Carl burst out laughing at her lighter and pulled out his own, a gold-plated Zippo which his Dad, Carl Senior, had given him when he was twelve, to celebrate his first lay. Carl's family was like that. Carl didn't think there was anything weird about them (though in truth he barely knew them: boarding school).

On producing the lighter, Carl adopted a stupid Aussie accent. Said: 'That's not a lighter. *This* is a lighter.' Aping fucking Paul Hogan in *Crocodile Dundee.* Sleazy bastard was forever quoting from movies. Sometimes I think films raised him more than his parents ever did. Made him the man he was.

None of the girls seemed to get the Hogan reference, which probably meant they were on the young side. But fair play to them, they none of them let Carl's stupid comment put them off. Not when they were so close to getting in to VIP.

Adam asked what they were called, and everything was OK after that. Adam could get a fucking *stone* to melt and give in, the good-looking bastard.

Their names were Natalie, Rachel and... I forget the other one.

Natalie latched herself onto me. She talked ten to the dozen and I barely listened to a word in three, but from what I could work out she called herself The Nat. Like she was a real one-off; the one and only. But she was just like every Natalie I'd ever met. Dyed blond hair, caked-on make-up. Ridiculous spray-tan. Great figure. Terrible Leeds accent. She tried to soften this when speaking to me, but sometimes the Yorkshire just slipped out of her.

Rachel went with Adam. Practically climbed inside his already tight tee she was on him so close. Honestly, she was like a brunette hermit crab. To be fair – and this used to be hard to admit; after all it's hardly the kind of thing you want to say about your close friends, especially in our... I suppose you'd call it a clique, which operated and balanced itself out on healthy doses of schadenfreude, piss-taking and banter – Adam *was* beautiful. I mean, he had a great big beauty spot the size of a fifty-pence piece on his cheek and on most people this would have been the worst kind of deformity, and, as soon as money happened their way the spot would have gone under the knife. But Adam wore it like a badge of honour: he'd been through rough times with it – kids can be all kinds of cruel – and come out the other end. Now women couldn't get enough of it. They thought it made him sympathetic. Mysterious. Full of hidden depths and pain. In effect, the spot kind of balanced out the effect of his bulging biceps and his cut chest and his square jaw, which was to make him a type of identikit beautiful, and elevated him to another plane: a *unique* kind of beauty. Everyone knew who Ads was.

(Hell, Rachel wasn't even put off by his clumsy chat. She was caught so off-guard by him I heard her introduce herself using her full name, like their meeting was some kind of job interview. 'Rachel Stonehouse,' she said. And Ads raised an eyebrow, like he does. Then proffered a paw. 'N'I'm Adam Penthouse. As in I live in one. As in, d'you wanna see it later?')

The other girl, the one I never caught the name of,

was the best of the bunch. She *was* stunning. Real Jewish princess type. Could have been a contender, or at least a winning contestant in *Big Brother*. She went with Carl, only, as soon as we'd been shown to a table and had our drinks order taken, she went off 'to powder her nose'. Never came back. Not to us. Turned out she'd had a better offer (or had sensed Carl's sleaziness). We saw her later on, dripping off the arm of a kid I thought might have been a boyband singer. Of course, we gave Carl all kinds of shit for her deserting him but he took this with good grace. Least we thought he did. What happened later *might just* have never occurred had the girl not used him just to get inside the VIP section and had we not hammered him with so much banter he should have been wearing a tin-hat.

So anyway, what we did was what we usually did. We lounged. We were cool as geckos. Carl, unreadable behind his mirror-shades. Sometimes you couldn't tell whether he was asleep behind them. But then he'd flick out a tongue and lick a girl's ear, or nibble on her shoulder, and get her to pour him another drink. (Already another girl had come over and replaced his Jewish princess). Adam more twitchy: he was caning it on the coke. But cool as fuck whatever because he had that first-man look about him and he could have pulled off a full-on eppie in here and still everyone would have wanted to be him. Me method-acting like crazy. Trying not to grin like a loon. All the while feeling like all kinds of a fraud (but a well-dressed one).

We were princes and this was our court: The Townhouse, Assembly Street, Leeds.

We were princes and this was our court: I kept telling myself that over and over and eventually it *sort of* materialised into truth, like, to use a Carl reference, when you said Beetlejuice enough times in the mirror. Well, hell, there were enough mirrors in this place. It was just about the most narcissistic bar in the world. It was all sheen and sparkle and minimalist and sterile. It bore about as much likeness to the pubs I'd grown up in that it might as well have been a spaceship. There wasn't so much as a single brass affixed to the wall (though there were a couple speakers tucked up in the corners which always struck me as looking a lot like those buckety, pod-shaped urinals we used to have in our Gents; Dad had installed little footballs in the well of them in order to assist the pissed-up old alcies to shoot straight).

We were sat in our own booth. It was always reserved for us. Might as well have stuck a plaque on it. Just far enough away to the bar so you didn't get jostled. Just close enough so you could catch one of the barmaid's eyes and get her to whip you up a quick cocktail or whatever. Other booths were filled-up with rock stars, soap starlets and footballers. We were on nodding terms with most of them. Carl had Rio Ferdinand's number in his contacts list on his Nokia, his gold Nokia which when you looked at it squint, he claimed looked a bit like C3PO. Said he could bell him – Rio, not Threepio - any time he wanted for comp tickets to Elland Road. Which was all kinds of funny because none of us would have been seen dead there.

Every night it was always the hardcore three of us, but there'd also be the hanger's-on too; sometimes we didn't even know their names, just their needy faces. We'd slap their hands away from the bottles - blueberry Stoli and strawberry Stoli - chilling in the ice buckets, and once Adam gave one of them a smack for having the termerity, the stupidity, to try to wipe off his beauty spot, believing it some kind of smudge, but occasionally we'd toss them our leavings, our leftovers: a girl who'd had too much to drink and who'd gotten all maudlin; a bottle which had gotten warm.

There were a number of these malingerers that night, the night Carl got the bouncers to beat seven shades of shit out of those two lads outside. One guy who looked like Toadfish out of *Neighbours* – hell maybe he *was* Toadfish out of *Neighbours;* a couple other Aussie soap stars had come over to guest in *Emmerdale* recently – was particularly annoying. He claimed to know Adam from the gym, but by the way Adam kept looking so quizzically at him, he might not have done. Mind you, Adam often forgot faces. And names. And other things too.

Toadfish was toadying up to us in all the worst ways. He kept trying to drag Adam off to the toilets, because he had the best 'Colombian Marching Powder' known to humanity. We kept telling him to keep his fucking voice down, Brains. He kept staring down The Nat's top, too, and bloody hell was that not on because *I* was the one paying for her bloody drinks so who was he to get a freeman's look-see? And he was annoying Carl just by being alive.

In the end Adam and I got rid of him by sending him over to the DJ to ask for *Kernkraft 400* by Zombie Nation. Reason we wanted of *Kernkraft 400* was kind of an in-joke. We hated it really and no DJ worth his salt would have spun such commercial bullshit. But Toadfish was all like, *yeah man, that's my favourite tune too!* So enthusiastic we all wanted to throw him out the window. In the end the DJ must have done our job for us because we never saw Toadfish again and we certainly never heard Zombie

Nation (though we did a few rounds of the zombie-walk dance from the video just to annoy Carl all the same).

Another fella kept pestering me for my phone number (must have been how Rio Ferdinand felt before he finally relented and gave his number to Carl). I had no idea *why* he wanted my number; just saw how desperately he wanted it. Which obviously made me absolutely desperate not to give him anything. Not even an acknowledgement of his presence. When he walked away, I heard him say something about me being 'a real dick', and had I been Adam, I might have gone after him. But I wasn't Adam, and besides, even though it was still the best of times, even I could see how dickishly we all behaved sometimes. So fair do's.

Still, it seemed the more dickish we were, the more everyone else presumed we were top-drawer people. In those days most of the people on the Calls, or in The Townhouse must have thought we were famous in some way or other — maybe they thought they'd seen Adam modelling smalls in *GQ*, or Carl playing some kind of lawyer in *Emmerdale* (despite all his efforts, there was definitely something sleazy about him: people could sense it), or me warming the subs bench for Leeds United - and we didn't bother trying to disabuse them of this notion.

And anyway, we *were* famous. In the right circles.

And anyway, we had money (some) so that was all that mattered.

The Nat and Rachel kept trying to find out what it was Adam and I did. Just so they could be sure the next morning when they texted their mates and told them 'Slept with a *whatever*' last night they had it right. Adam tried to spin some yarn about being a famous artist, the next Damien Hirst, but neither of the girls knew who Damien Hirst was so his story was dead in the water. Probably a good job. He was babbling all kinds of nonsense by that point – a couple times even lapsing into Polish, which he spoke with his parents – and his legs were juddering up and down like pistons under the table, so for anyone to even consider he might be able to hold a paintbrush or a sculptor's chisel or whatever might have been a leap too far. He was drinking like a fish, too. Coke made him do that. Speed made him even faster. Even though the rest of us had barely touched our drinks, Ads was already reaching into the bucket and pulling out the bottle, ice and water slewing off it, tipping it over his own glass once again.

And again: *na zdrowie*. Down the hatch.

'So what *are* you?' The Nat was pressing me now, in more ways than one. I felt her leg hard against mine.

I just told The Nat she didn't want to know, love. If I told her what we really did, she'd want to punch me hard, right in the solar plexus. Or else her eyes would roll back in her head and she'd slip into some somnambulist state. Sleep for a hundred years. When we talked about what we did for a living (or should that have been dying?) it often had that effect.

The Nat asked me where my accent was from. I told her it was from the same place as me.

She pouted. 'Ha-ha. Where are *you* from then, Mister Comedian?'

I told her I was from London. I was a spy, working for MI5.

She rolled her eyes and poured herself another drink.

I was already growing bored with her. I looked over at Carl. The girl sat with him appeared to have changed again – unless she'd done her hair different in the toilets – and he seemed to be having a bit more luck with her. He caught me looking and reached over for the ice bucket. He picked out an ice cube and he ran it all the way up her leg and then under the hem of her (very) short skirt. She squealed and Carl winked at me, sleazily.

Then The Nat squealed too, and for a moment I

thought she'd done so because she'd also been watching Carl's ice-cube show and maybe she was either disgusted or turned on by it. Who knew?

But when I swung round to her, I saw she wasn't even looking in Carl's direction. Instead she was looking off to the right, where some sort of commotion was taking place at the top of the stairs. The bouncer with the captain's armband was trying to hold back two immensely angry-looking, and *tough*-looking lads. You could tell from the start these lads weren't cut out for the VIP section. They'd dressed *okay*, but their gear wasn't *quite* in season. Shirt, trousers and shoes were TK Maxx specials if ever I saw them. They looked the type to have *paid* for their booty by stealing tools from the backs of white vans, or else raiding other people's garden sheds; selling on the loot on the black market in shitty, dead-end pubs like the one I grew up in. Their haircuts weren't right either. Frankly they looked as though they'd tried too hard when they didn't have the beans in the first place.

We saw that kind of thing all the time up here.

The Nat clearly hadn't though. All the blood ran to her orange, spray-tanned face and she began slipping down in her seat. I tried to tell her everything would be okay; the bouncer would sort this; obviously he had something about him if he was wearing that luminous armband (even if I didn't know the guy personally, I knew other upper-echelon SAS and they were a cut above, truly). But she ignored me completely. She was practically kneeling on the floor now, in what Carl would have called 'optimum blowjob position'. She jabbed her finger into her friend Rachel's calf, then hissed: '*look*'.

Find out what happens in the rest of the novel by visiting A.J. Kirby's official blog-site: https://paintthistownred.wordpress.com/

ABOUT THE AUTHOR

AJ Kirby is the author of the novels *The Sleep of Reason Produces Monsters, When Elephants walk through the Gorbals, Paint this Town Red, Bully, Perfect World* and *Sharkways*.

His short fiction has been published across the web, and in magazines, anthologies and literary journals, as well as in three collections: *Trickier & Treatier, The Art of Ventriloquism* and *Mix Tape*.

He was one of 20 Leeds-based authors under 40 recently shortlisted for the LS13 competition and his novel Paint this Town Red was shortlisted for The Guardian's Not the Booker prize.

He reviews fiction for The New York Journal of Books and The Short Review.

In addition he has written three books about Manchester United: *Louis van Gaal: Dutch Courage, The Pride of All Europe: Manchester United's Greatest Seasons in the European Cup,* and *Fergie's Finest: Sir Alex Ferguson's Greatest Manchester United x11.*

His official website is here:
http://www.andykirbythewriter.20m.com/
And he blogs here:
http://paintthistownred.wordpress.com/

CHECK OUT THESE OTHER AJ KIRBY PUBLICATIONS BROUGHT TO YOU BY WHITE HOUSE PRESS

'WHEN ELEPHANTS WALK THROUGH THE GORBALS' BY AJ KIRBY

When Elephants Walk Through the Gorbals is a gritty thriller, set in 1970s Glasgow, involving a close-to-the-edge detective, a suicidal journalist, five murders and a young art student's chance meeting with a stranger on a train which draws him into the heart of darkness of the city.

Against the backdrop of the decaying city, the characters are pushed inexorably towards a dramatic, nail-biting finale after which nothing will ever be the same again.

The novel won third-prize in won third place in the Luke Bitmead Memorial Bursary, run by Legend Press – following such luminaries as Sophie Duffy, and Andrew Blackman onto the podium – and has been extensively revised since its success in the competition.

At a time when Scottish devolution has become headline news, this mystery/ crime thriller set in a not so bonny Scotland explores many of the key themes.

'THE SLEEP OF REASON PRODUCES MONSTERS' BY AJ KIRBY

Roll up, roll up for the magical mystery tour of the museum of sleep, a place where your dreams can stand up and walk, just the same as your nightmares.

Charlie Prince and his father are looking for a little adventure at the weekend. They want to escape their real-world problems for a few hours. But they get a lot more than they bargained for when they visit the new museum in town. For here the exhibits are much more monstrous than the ones they face at home.

Soon Charlie discovers they are trapped inside the museum, and they are not alone. Monsters lurk in the dark corners, twitching to hunt them down. A trio of bears thunder after them in a frenzied pursuit. A mischievous not-quite-white rabbit promises to help them but ends up luring them into his lair.

And behind them all, the sinister puppet-master Howard Cunliffe lies in wait, eager to trap Charlie inside forever.

Channelling Lewis Carroll, Edgar Allan Poe and Stephen King, this subtly dark, surreal story will ensure you'll sleep with the light on tonight.

AND, FROM OUR GHOST STORIES SERIES…

'HANGINGSTONE' BY AJ KIRBY

'Hangingstone' is a supernatural tale of madness, motherhood, and revenge.

Set on the wild Yorkshire moorland near Ilkley, it is the story of one mother's desperate attempts to reconcile herself with the (ghostly) child who was taken from her many years ago.

Hangingstone Rocks are two monoliths of millstone grit which look out upon the seemingly idyllic town of Ilkley, a place which has stored up a wealth of terrible memories, particularly in its treatment of our less than fortunate mother, who returns to the rocks again and again in order to try and find a way back into the past, to the moment her child was taken away from her.

By the Amazon top-selling dark fiction author of 'Bully', 'Sharkways', 'Paint this town Red', 'The Black Book', and 'The Haunting of Annie Nicol'.

ALSO FROM WHITE HOUSE PRESS…

'KIDNEY PUNCH' BY ANDY JACOBI

WINNER OF THE WHITE HOUSE PRESS FIRST NOVEL AWARD 2014

Shane Jackett is a fighter, born and bred.
He's had to fight for everything, all his life.
It is all he knows how to do.

But when his family is threatened to be torn apart for a second time, Shane faces a terrible choice.

Unflinching in its honesty, and often brutal in its outlook, 'Kidney Punch' is the story of Shane's coming to terms with his own masculinity in a world where there are a severe lack of adequate role models.

It's a story about men escaping from responsibility, through drinking, fighting, running away.

It's about trying to do the right thing when things get so bad it is not even clear what the right thing is.

This is the first novel by North-West England-based author, ANDY JACOBI, and it is already garnering high-praise from critics.

AND, FROM OUR 'NEW MYTHS' SERIES…

'MR. 0' BY AINE J. CABAYE

Vinny Markham and his gang of mates are troubled.
They have discovered their new neighbour might have
a very dark past.
And they don't know what to do about it.
But they know they should do something.

But with their only role-models the itinerant fathers
they are at once ashamed and in awe of, there is
something inevitable about the dark, destructive, and
lawless nature of the boys' response.

Recalling Graham Greene's 'The Destructors', and
William Golding's 'The Lord of the Flies', Aine
Cabaye's dystopian short story about the destructive
power of evil transports Homer's 'Odyssey' to a
modern-day estate in the north east of England.

Author Aine J. Cabaye is half-Irish, half-French, and
lives halfway between Leeds and Hull, in the north east
of England. She is the parent of one child, Noel, and
of four books, the first two of which are to be
published by White House Press.

AND, FROM OUR 'NEW MYTHS' SERIES...

'LEAPER' BY AJK SUTHERLAND

When you take the plunge, they say, your whole life
flashes before your eyes.
The highs, the lows.

In the original myth of Icarus, the eponymous hero
was warned not to fly too close to the sun, for fear that
the wax which attached his wings to him might melt.
In AJK Sutherland's tale, it is all the trappings of the
21st century which melt, and our Icarus is left to
contemplate his life as a failure, with no hope of
redemption.

Only a small, scruffy dog might save him... But is it too
late, as he balances on the edge of the bridge, looking
out on his death.

'Leaper' is the third novelette of the Classic Myths
Reinvented series from White House Press. Taking as
its inspiration the mythical character of 'Icarus', AJK
Sutherland's tragic tale of failed ambition and hubris is
"a tear-a-minute writing" (The Book Shelf Reviews)
which "soars to the heights of mania, before plunging
to the depths of depression... sometimes within the
same sentence." (The Bar-Room Literary Critic).

AND, FROM OUR 'NEW MYTHS' SERIES...

'MOTHER NATURE' BY JAMES HENRY KIER

The second in the White House Press 'New Myths' series is the fantastic 'Mother Nature' by James Henry Kier.

"I wake up and my head feels like a broken dog biscuit."

So begins our descent into our 21st century 'Persephone's' world. In Greek myth Persephone was Queen of the Underworld, only, in Kier's story, that underworld is very much the world we know.

For hers is a world of casual drug use and even more casual sex. Text messages. Alcohol.

And a custody battle with her erstwhile partner which threatens to tear her world apart.

AND, FROM OUR 'NEW MYTHS' SERIES…

'THE UNION OF WATER BEARERS' BY DREW CUBBY

Water, water, nowhere. And not a drop to drink. Welcome to the near future world of Nick End, an architect at the End of Days.

In Nick's world water is the most valuable commodity there is. For most, there is no clean water at all, only synthetic energy drinks.

But when Nick stumbles across ghostly figures dripping across the screens which broadcast CCTV images, he inadvertently splashes right into a quest to discover what happened to all the water. And it is a story which begins to tell him a great deal about himself, and why he is the way he is. So dry. So desert, desert dry.

32290768R00026

Printed in Great Britain
by Amazon